HELPERS IN OUR COMMUNITY

CONSTRUCTION WORKERS

CHRISTINE HONDERS

New York

Published in 2020 by The Rosen Publishing Group, Inc.
29 East 21st Street, New York, NY 10010

Copyright © 2020 by The Rosen Publishing Group, Inc.

All rights reserved. No part of this book may be reproduced in any form without permission in writing from the publisher, except by a reviewer.

First Edition

Editor: Greg Roza
Book Design: Reann Nye

Photo Credits: Cover, p.1 Don Mason/Getty Images; pp. 4–22 Abstractor/Shutterstock.com; p. 5 Purit Lertsri/Shutterstock.com; p. 7 VanderWolf Images/Shutterstock.com; p. 9 LightField Studios/Shutterstock.com; p. 11 Stockr/Shutterstock.com; p. 13 Halfpoint/Shutterstock.com; p. 15 BraunS/E+/Getty Images; p. 17 kali9/E+/Getty Images; p. 19 antpkr/Shutterstock.com; p. 21 Hero Images/Getty Images; p. 22 kurhan/Shutterstock.com.

Library of Congress Cataloging-in-Publication Data
Names: Honders, Christine.
Title: Construction workers / Christine Honders.
Description: New York : PowerKids Press, 2020. | Series: Helpers in our community | Includes glossary and index.
Identifiers: ISBN 9781725308183 (pbk.) | ISBN 9781725308206 (library bound) | ISBN 9781725308190 (6 pack)
Subjects: LCSH: Construction workers–Juvenile literature.
Classification: LCC TH149.H66 2020 | DDC 624-dc23

Manufactured in the United States of America

CPSIA Compliance Information: Batch #CWPK20. For Further Information contact Rosen Publishing, New York, New York at 1-800-237-9932.

CONTENTS

Who Put That There? 4
What Is a
    Construction Worker? 6
Jack of All Trades 8
Special Skills 10
Danger on the Job 12
Construction Tools 14
Safety First! 16
Rain or Shine 18
Working as a Team 20
Building Better Communities . 22
Glossary 23
Index 24
Websites 24

Who Put That There?

What do you see when you walk outside in your town? There are buildings. There are streets. Maybe a store or your school is down the street. We use roads and buildings every day. They make our lives easier. We can thank construction workers for putting them there!

What Is a Construction Worker?

"Construction" means the act of building something. Construction workers build and fix roads, bridges, houses, and other buildings. Construction workers use many things that come from Earth. They use sand and rocks to make **concrete**. They use **iron** to make steel. Steel is a strong metal that keeps buildings from falling over!

concrete

Jack of All Trades

Construction workers do many things. They carry building supplies to and from the job. They build **scaffolds** around buildings. This makes it easier for them to work. Some construction workers tear down buildings. Others dig tunnels for roads.

scaffolding

Special Skills

Some construction workers have special skills. Some workers pour concrete to make **foundations** for buildings. Masons build with bricks or stone. Ironworkers use steel beams. Glaziers are workers who fit glass for windows into buildings. Some construction workers lay **asphalt** to build roads.

Danger on the Job

Construction workers sometimes face danger on the job. Sometimes, they blow up old buildings. They work high in the air on skyscrapers. They dig underground tunnels. Some construction workers make buildings safe. They remove dangerous stuff, such as **asbestos**, that can make people sick.

Construction Tools

Construction workers use hand tools such as shovels and hammers. They also use power tools. They may use jackhammers to break up concrete! They have special drills to make tunnels. They drive trucks and bulldozers for digging and for moving dirt.

Safety First!

Construction workers don't want to get hurt. They wear goggles, hard hats, and gloves. They wear brightly colored vests so people will see them working at night. Some construction tools are loud! Construction workers wear ear plugs to keep their ears safe.

Rain or Shine

Our communities need new buildings and roads all the time. Construction workers can't wait for good weather. They work in the heat or in the cold. They don't stop when it rains. No matter what's going on outside, they have a job to finish.

Working as a Team

Houses need roofs, lights, bathrooms, and a lot more! That's why construction workers need to work as a team. Construction workers help with anything the team needs. They set up and fix tools. They clean up when the job is done.

Building Better Communities

We owe a lot to construction workers. They make our buildings safe. They fix roads that get us from place to place. They're the reason we have a place to go home at night. Construction workers make our community a great place to live!

GLOSSARY

asbestos: A material that doesn't burn but can make people very sick.

asphalt: A dark building material used to make roads.

concrete: A hard, strong building material made by mixing cement, sand, broken rocks, and water.

foundation: The base a house is built on.

iron: A heavy silver metal found in many rocks.

scaffold: A platform that supports workers while they build.

INDEX

A
asbestos, 12
asphalt, 10

C
concrete, 6, 10, 14

F
foundations, 10

G
glaziers, 10

H
hammers, 14

I
iron, 6, 10

M
masons, 10

S
scaffolds, 8
shovels, 14
steel, 6, 10

T
tools, 14, 16, 20
tunnels, 8, 12

WEBSITES

Due to the changing nature of Internet links, PowerKids Press has developed an online list of websites related to the subject of this book. This site is updated regularly. Please use this link to access the list: www.powerkidslinks.com/HIOC/construction